What Time Is It?

Laron Davis

Rosen REAL READERS

Rosen Classroom Books & Materials
New York

What time is it?

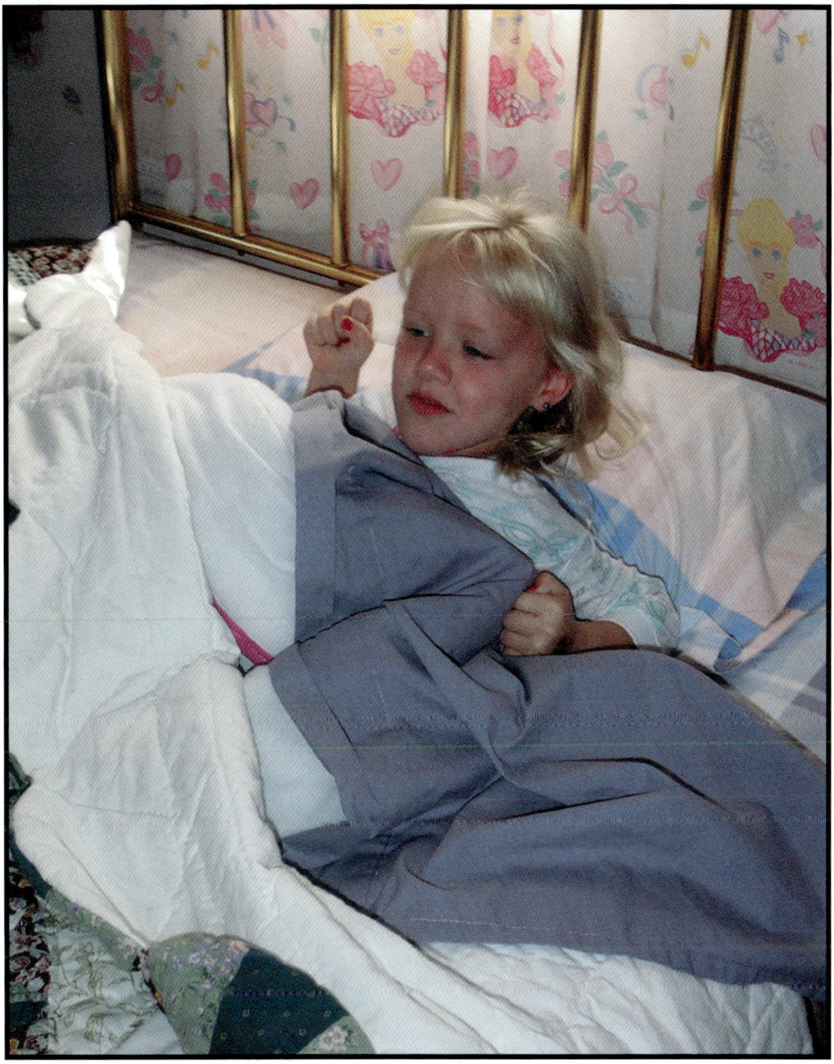

It is time to get up.

It is time to eat breakfast.

It is time to go to school.

It is time to eat lunch.

It is time to go home.

Words to Know

breakfast

lunch

school